The Case of
The Missing Baseball Cards

The Case of
The Missing Baseball Cards

Ruth Zakutinsky

AURA PRESS
88 Parkville Avenue / Brooklyn, NY 11230

The Case of the Missing Baseball Cards

ISBN 0-911643-01-X

Printed in the U.S.A.

Published by
AURA PRESS, INC.
88 Parkville Avenue
Brooklyn, New York 11230
(718) 435-9103

One

Suddenly, Mrs. Diamond woke up. Who was prowling around downstairs? She sat up in bed and listened. Someone *was* rummaging through cabinets and pulling open drawers — and it was still dark outside, not even dawn. Should she telephone the police? Or was it just. . .

"Yosef!"

"Yosef!" She called to her nine-year old son. "What are you doing down there?"

"Mom! I can't find them!" Yosef ran urgently upstairs. "I can't find them, Mom, — the esrogim* that Judah and Yoni brought home last night. I can't sleep anymore. Where *are* they?"

I would like to sleep some more! thought Mrs. Diamond. "On top of the refrigerator!" she said to him, hoping he would be quiet now so that she could sleep for another half hour.

Yosef raced downstairs and screeched a kitchen chair across the linoleum. Ten seconds later, he was charging upstairs again, this time toward his older brother Judah's room. The door crashed open as he hurried in.

"Judah! Tell me! Which one is mine?"

"Wha'?" Judah started, as a sharp cardboard edge scraped his nose.

*also pronounced etrogim — plural for etrog

"Are you crazy? Get those esrog boxes off my chin and let me sleep!"

"But I have to know which is mine!" said Yosef, as he hastily, but carefully, took a large, yellow esrog fruit from one of the boxes. "Is this one Daddy's?"

"Uh?" Judah looked up sleepily. "Yes, that's Daddy's."

"But this one," urged Yosef, taking hold of a little esrog, which looked like a small bumpy green lemon. "This little icky one isn't *mine,* is it?"

"It *isn't* icky," sighed Judah, pulling the pillow over his head.

"It's icky and *green!*" insisted Yosef, his lower lip trembling.

"No it's *not!*" Judah came out from under the pillow. It was no use, Yosef wouldn't let him alone. "Look, Yosef," he explained to his younger brother, "This is a perfect esrog. Believe me, it is kosher. There is nothing wrong with it. It is green because it was green when they picked it off the tree. Like oranges," Judah continued sleepily. "Oranges also are green, not orange, when they are picked. So go downstaires now, okay, and let me sleep!"

"Next year I want to go with you to help pick out my own!" Yosef insisted. "And now I *better* go downstairs, to see what kind of *lulov,* the palm branches, that you bought." Yoseph leaped down the stairs, slamming the door behind him.

"No! I don't believe it!" Yosef's piercing scream echoed through the house, as he raced up to Judah's room. "It's

dried up, Judah!" Yosef was almost in tears. "This lulov is all dried out! Just look at these leaves! They are coming apart!"

"Ummph!" Judah had almost fallen back to sleep.

"Dry!" repeated Yosef. "And it isn't straight up to the tip and tight the way we learned it was supposed to be. Anyway, this is a small one!"

"Uhh?" Judah yawned. "A leaf is all it needs. A small palm leaf wrapped around it to make it tight keeps lulov leaves from spreading. Okay? I'll take care of it."

"Well, if you don't, then I want to switch!"

"And *I* want to sleep!" warned Judah. "Now out! Stop waking up the whole house!"

"It's already awake," yawned Shoni, the boy's fourteen year old sister, as she came out of her room brushing her hair.

Yoni, who was seventeen, was also already out of bed. He came downstairs to the kitchen, stretching and rubbing his eyes. "What's this racket?" he asked. "Can't a person sleep around here?"

"With *him* around here?" Judah, who had given up on falling back to sleep, joined Yoni in the kitchen. The two older brothers glanced over to the kitchen table, where Yosef was earnestly assembling the three varieties of branches for the lulov.

"What are you doing?" questioned Yoni. "Look Yosef, just take those myrtle twigs, the 'hadassim,' and those willow twigs, the 'aravos'* and put them back where you

---

*'aravos' also pronounced arovot

3

found them, okay?"

"But tomorrow is Sukkos"*, urged Yosef. "I want them to be ready!"

"They have to be fresh. Do us all a favor and just put them back in the refrigerator."

Yosef reluctantly wrapped them in dampened newspaper and put them back in the refrigerator above the vegetable bin. "At least I can put my esrog in my olivewood box from Israel," he said. He gently lifted the esrog from its white cardboard box. The fragrant esrog was surrounded by soft, light, brown flax, which always reminded Yosef of a long, fake beard. Yosef looked at the esrog. It was a very delicate fruit. Its skin was tough, but at the end, opposite the stem, was a dry brownish little blossom called the "pitom", which could very easily break or fall off. If that happened, it couldn't be used. He carefully lined the olivewood box with the soft flax, and gently placed his esrog inside. "Remember that my esrog is already *in* my olivewood box, so no one touch it!" he cautioned his older brothers.

Judah and Yoni were not especially listening. Usually they had a lot of patience for their younger brother, especially now that they were away at Yeshiva. But this morning. . . well, enough was enough already. Last night, they had come home very late from the city, where they had gone to select the lulovim and esrogim, and also to pick up extra lumber for the sukkah. They had hoped to catch up on a little sleep this morning — but they were already

*also pronounced Sukkot

up and it wasn't even 6:30. Yoni opened the refrigerator, looking for the juice, and Judah reached for some glasses. They might as well catch the early *minyon* services at the shul* and start the day.

"Hey Yoni," piped in Yosef, "will we start the sukkah soon? Ask me anything you want to know about a sukkah. We learned it in class and I memorized it all in Hebrew. Listen, 'Sukkah, she he gvoha me esrim am ah: psulah.' — A sukkah, that-is-bigger-than-twenty-cubits, IS NOT TO BE USED."

Judah, who overheard this, had a one-track mind. "Can we ask you *anything* we want to know about sleep?"

"—What?" asked Yosef, caught off guard.

"A PER-son," chanted Judah, in the same chant Yosef had used, "who wakes-up-another-person-from-his-SLEEeep,-is-considered-*worse-than-a* THIEF!"

"Wha'—why?" asked Yosef, taken aback.

"Be-CAUSE," continued Judah, "a THIEeef can return the property that he stole. But one who a-WAKens another from his SLEEP, can *never* return the hours of sleep that that person lost!"

"Oy-glunk!" exclaimed Yosef, his face turning red, as he slapped one hand against his cheek. "Worse than a thief! And I bet I woke up the whole house today. . ." Yosef slumped down on a kitchen chair, strangely quiet. His mind seemed split in two. With half his mind, he was trying to figure out a way that maybe sleep *could* be paid back. And, at the same time, the awful scene at school

*synagogue

5

yesterday, with David and Ari, kept creeping into his mind. . . and what he did was worse than that. . .!

"We might as well catch the early-bird minyon," Judah's voice interrupted the wretched scenario that Yoseph didn't want to think about anyway.

"I'm coming too," Yosef said.

Two

It's a good thing 9½-year-olds can't drive, thought Judah, as Yosef chimed in again and nudged. "Can't you go faster, Judah? Hurry and step on it! We'll be late!"

Judah turned into the roadway and eased the Taylor into third gear. "I'm already going the speed-limit, not to mention the Taylor's limit," he replied. Judah smiled as he remembered a joke that he and Yoni used to have when they were about Yosef's age. "Why is our car called a "Taylor?" "Because it takes *sew* long to get there (ha, ha)."

"Why don't you just be quiet Yosef, and amuse your self in the backseat while we drive to shul?" suggested Yoni.

"Well, okay," said Yosef, a little reluctantly until he remembered that he had some of his baseball cards stuffed into his back pocket. He pulled them out and settled back to study the fact sheets on the backs of them. But he couldn't concentrate. The cards reminded him of yesterday, and again the thought of Ari and David tormented him. He couldn't divert his attention this time, and as he thought about it, it seemed even more real and awful then when it had happened.

It all started during recess, when he had been playing baseball in the school yard with his friends.

"Choose teams and I'll be right back. I'll go get my other mitt," Yosef had called to his friends.

His mitt was under his desk, so he ran back to the classroom. He could hardly believe it. There were David and Ari standing by Michael's desk, taking and opening packs of baseball cards.

"What are you doing?" Yosef had questioned them. "Those cards are Michael's."

"You better not tell or we'll beat you up," David snarled. He made a fist and took a few steps toward Yosef. "Not fair!" He grabbed his mitt and escaped from the room.

He ran back to his teammates but his legs didn't seem to be able to hold him straight. "Come on, Yosef, don't you want to play?" Jonathan had called. Then in the outfield, he had muffed one ball after another. This wasn't like him. Even the eighth graders always wanted him on their team. Yosef tried to concentrate, but coudn't. . . all he saw was David threatening him and making a fist.

"What's with you, Yos? Wake up!" Danny had yelled. "You keep muffing every ball!" Yosef pushed the gruesome thoughts out of his mind, so he would not let his team down, I'll think about it later, he said to himself. He concentrated with all his efforts and caught a pop fly.

"You're out and we're up!" yelled Michael. "Okay, Yos, you're up," Michael said, pointing at him. Yosef

gritted his teeth and waited for just the right pitch. SLAM
— "Go, go, go," he heard his teammates shout as he ran
around the bases. Danny patted him on the back as he slid
into home plate. "Knew you could do it! Now at least we
tied the score two to two."

Back in class Yosef couldn't think of the math assign-
ment on the board in front of him. David and Ari were
doing their work as if nothing had happened. Yosef
couldn't look at them, although he knew they were
glancing at him. He pretended not to notice, although he
felt them watching his every move. He had never been
best friends with either of them, but now. . .

And then came the dreadful moment when Michael
discovered that the cards were missing.

"Mrs. Snow! Someone took all the cards out of the
packs I brought to school. I can't find them!"

"Are you sure, Michael!? Why don't you go to all the
classes and ask the teachers if you can ask if anyone
knows what happened to them?"

"Even if I do find them, no one is going to buy opened
packs."

"Don't worry about that now," said Mrs. Snow, trying
to reasure him. "Let's just see if you can find them."

He didn't of course. Yosef moved uncomfortably in the
back seat, remembering how he saw David and Ari go into
the locker room together after school. Yosef had followed
them. His hunch was right. Of course, they were keeping
the cards hidden in their lockers. He could see that they

were huddled together, and it looked as if they were sorting and counting them.

There was no one else in the locker room. Ari looked up and saw Yosef standing and watching. He nudged David. Yosef said, "G-d sees, He's watching." David looked up and saw that the locker room was empty, except for Yosef. David sneered at Yosef.

"Here's Mr. Yosef, the goody-goody," he said sarcastically. "You're always so religious. Well, you better watch it or you're gonna get it!" He and Ari took a menacing step toward Yosef, but he ran out before they could lay a hand on him.

Now, back in the back seat of the car, he again felt the anger and burning frustration. "Goody-goody!" thought Yosef. "So religious! Humph! Those thieves!"

Just then Yoni, thinking it strange that his younger brother should be *so* quiet turned around. "Quiet is one thing, but you don't have to freeze up." He saw that his younger brother was upset about something. "What's wrong, Yos? Hey," Yoni continued, trying to cheer him up. "I see you have baseball cards."

Yosef only groaned at the reminder. He didn't want to go into the whole thing with Yoni, but he really did want to talk to someone. An earlier incident with David and Ari crossed his mind. He could talk about *that* anyway.

"It's these two guys at school," he began, "ever since I've come to this school, they have given me a real pain."

"Yeah?" said Yoni, "What do they do?"

"Well," Yosef continued, "it all started the first day at school, after we moved to Bridgeport. It was during recess, and I was at the water fountain, when I heard these two wise guys snickering, 'Hey kid, your strings are sticking out!' They were talking to me! I could hardly believe it when I saw them there pointing at me and laughing. We go to a Hebrew Day school, so what are they making such a big fuss about my *tzitzis* fringes* for? Even if they didn't know, from home, they teach us at school why we should wear them. I've been wearing mine since I'm three."

"Sure," said Yoni. "Well, it just shows how much they know. They should have been on the battlefield when the Israelis were fighting the Egyptians during the Six-Day War. Then they would know what tzitzis are all about."

"Yeah?" asked Yosef. "How is that?"

"Remember Chaim Rubin, the Israeli soldier who was visiting us last year? He told me that he and his whole tank crew were saved during the war because he was wearing tzitzis."

"What happened?" asked Yosef.

"They were in the middle of the battlefield," began Yoni, "in the desert, on a day that was hotter from shell-blasts then it was from the sun. There were four of them in the tank. They had been out on the Egyptian front, and were heading back for more ammunition. They were going at top speed, of course, but suddenly they were hit by an Egyptian shell and their tank careened out of commission,

---

*Religious undergarment worn by males called Talis Katan — small Talis.

in a real no-parking zone! Their only hope was to make it safely on foot to the Israeli lines. So they quickly scrambled out and started running. Then, they spotted an Israeli tank in the distance ahead of them. You would think that would have been good news. The only problem was that the Israeli tank had its gun pointed toward *them,* thinking they were Egyptian infantry! What a spot to be in! The enemy behind them, and their countrymen in front of them, but thinking that *they* were the enemy! They didn't know what to do. How could they let the Israelis know not to shoot — that they also were Israelis? Suddenly, Chaim took off his shirt. His friends thought he was going crazy. But then he took off his tzitzis and began waving them in the air like a flag. When the Israeli tank commander spotted *that* through his sight lens, he called to the gunner, "Hold fire! Those must be our guys! No Egyptian would be wearing tzitzis!"

"That story's okay!" Yosef smiled at Yoni. The Taylor chugged to a halt. They had reached the shul.

Three

When the boys entered, many of the men were already
there preparing to pray. They nodded greetings to Judah
and Yoni, but when they saw Yosef, many of the men
welcomed him with a big smile, and some even patted him
on the back.

"How do they know *you* so well?" asked Judah.

"I bike up here a lot of times to services before school,"
Yosef answered, "they don't care if I'm not thirteen yet."

Judah and Yoni smiled. "Everyone has to wait thirteen
years to be thirteen. Your day will come."

Yosef sighed, as he watched Judah and Yoni join the
other men who were getting ready for prayer. He watched
them remove the *tephilin* from their velvet bags. They
unwound the long, black, leather straps and wound them
carefully around their arms, precisely centering the
"Battim," the little boxes that contain the special Torah
passages, one on their left forearm and then the other
adjusting it on their heads. Yosef eyed them. He would be
bar mitzvahed too, some day, and then he too, would be
able to wear his own pair. Well, they are worth waiting
for. Yosef had already looked deeply into the matter, and
he could tell anyone who asked, or even who didn't ask,

what was involved.

As he watched the men wind the tephilin, Yosef remembered a story that his teacher, Rabbi Golder, had told the class about tephilin. It was about Rabbi Elisha,* long ago in Jerusalem, just before the second Temple was destroyed. Jerusalem was already under the control of the Romans, who were very mean to the Jews. The Romans said they would kill any Jew who they caught doing certain commandments. Among the commandments which were forbidden was the *mitzvah*-commandmant of tephilin,

"Whoever places tephilin on their head will have their brains pierced!" the Romans decreed.

This didn't stop Rabbi Elisha. He put on his tephilin and walked in the streets of the market place, just as though the decree had never been issued. A Roman soldier saw him and, of course, chased him. Through the streets they ran, until the soldier finally cornered Rabbi Elisha in an alley. "What have you there?" the soldier gruffly demanded. By this time, Rabbi Elisha had taken the tephilin in his hands. He turned to the soldier and bravely declared. "The wings of a dove!"

And when he opened his hands, a miracle occurred — a dove escaped and soared upward.

The soldier was stunned, and Rabbi Elisha escaped unharmed. But why did he say "wings of a dove?" Because, Yosef's rabbi had explained, the Jews are compared to doves. Just as a dove protects itself by its

*Also known as "Master of the Wings."

wings, so do the mitzvos that Jews observe protect them, giving them "wings" to soar, to escape from harm.

Yosef eyed the tephilin again. The boxes of the tephilin, when the straps are wound up, look like *tanks,* he thought to himself. Well, I sure wish I had some tephilin — tanks with me the next time I have to deal with David and Ari.

Yosef opened a *sidur*-prayer book, and tried to clear some room in his mind so that he could pray.

It wasn't easy. David, Ari and Michael kept creeping in during his praying. He went through several pages until he realized that what he was "praying" was actually a scheme as to how he could open up David's locker and give the cards back to Michael. He pushed those thoughts out of his mind and tried to concentrate on the words.

"Master of the Universe! It is not because of our good deeds that we stand before you, but because of Your abundant mercies!" Well, that was for sure. He imagined that he had just opened David's locker. There were the cards! But suddenly from out of nowhere, David and Ari came at him. A flying tackle! "Two against one isn't fair!" shouts Michael, and the whole class suddenly begins to shout. . .

"Blessed is He who spoke and the world came into being!" Yosef quickly rose to his feet and tried to concentrate again. Tomorrow was Sukkos. Tomorrow? No! It begins tonight. Tonight it begins! And their sukkah wasn't even up yet, much less decorated. The chairs had to be put in, and the table. Were they going to be crowded like last year? Last year, their table was so crowded in that little sukkah, that you had to keep your elbows in front of you, up against your stomach. That's why Judah and Yoni went into town yesterday, to get more lumber to make the sukkah bigger. Lumber! They never had a wood sukkah before. As long as Yosef could remember, they had had a canvas one. Lumber was much better. The canvas ones never staked in right. They always *thought* they did. Last year, a big gust of wind lifted it up like a balloon and let it down right in the middle of the street, in front of their house. *That* was some Sukkos. . .

"Yehay She-may Rabbah! — May His name be made great!"

They were up to *kaddish* already? Yosef shook his head and tried to concentrate on the meanings of the words in front of him. His rabbi always said that when strange thoughts come to your mind during prayers, you have to just push them away. You just have to keep fighting against that urge inside of you that makes you think about the wrong things when you are trying to pray. "It happens to all of us," Yosef's rabbi had said, "so just push away the thoughts, and go back to praying. That is one of the reasons prayer is called "avodah," which means "work" — because making yourself concentrate on the prayer, and really thinking about Who we're praying to, and to thank Him, and realize how great He is, and to ask Him for the things that we need. . . to do all that instead of just thinking whatever little thought happens to come to your mind, that's really hard work. "Just try to think about the meaning of each word, and *don't* give up. . ." That's what his rabbi had told them. He was probably so good at praying by now that he probably didn't even *have* any strange distracting thoughts in *his* mind any more. . .

"SHEMA YISROEL. . ."

Already up to Shema? Yosef quickly covered his eyes. "Shemah Yisroel Hashem Elokeynu Hashem Ehhh-Chhaaad! He is the only One in all the heavens and the four corners of the earth!" Yosef got his thoughts right that time. There is something about the Shema that seems to yank you out from whatever you were thinking and puts your mind in the right place.

And so, Yosef continued praying until he reached the Shemona Esrai, the holiest prayer, where you are supposed to be actually standing before your maker. Really standing right in front of Him, with your list of all the things that you want to ask Him. Can you imagine standing in front of a king? Or maybe the President of the United States? Or Ron Glazer, the pitcher, maybe? And he was there, looking at you, and waiting for you to ask Him whatever you want to ask Him. So what would you do? Would you waste your time thinking about crazy things, or would you get to the point? Yosef looked down and noticed that he had already reached more than halfway through the Shemona Esrai and he had been thinking about kings, presidents and pitchers. He broke into a cold sweat.

Please help me to pray to You! Help me to think about what I'm supposed to think about, and please help me to figure out what to do with David and Ari.

There, that was everything. Yosef was behind everyone in his prayers. He didn't care. So he would be the last one finished. So what? He was the youngest one there. Let them think he was just slow in his reading, but he was going to say the rest with the best concentration that he could. And he did. Walking out of shul, he heard one of the men say that he heard on the radio this morning, that a thief got loose from the state prison in New York and might come prowling around this way.

Four

Yosef could tell that, even though the men smiled at those remarks and wished each other a "happy holiday," the possibility of a 'loose thief' was making everyone feel uneasy.

"Is it true?" Yosef asked his brothers, as they got into the wagon. "Is there a thief, who escaped from the state prison, lurking around here?"

Judah and Yoni looked at each other. To get Yosef more excited than he usually was, was the last thing that they needed.

"Look Yosef," said Judah, "the guy has probably been caught by now. And even if he hasn't been caught, why would he want to stay around here? He could be anywhere in the world by now."

"Maybe. . ." said Yosef uncertainly. He took out his baseball cards and began to shuffle them, his mind on the thief. Well, thinking about it wouldn't catch him. "Want to flip, Yoni?" he said to his brother.

"In the *car?*"

"Sure, I've got the whole back seat. Do you want to see how many cards I have? There are only a few, really. I've got lots more at home." Yosef stacked the cards on the armrest of the stationwagon, and passed his back pocket samples up to Yoni.

"Humm, not bad," commented Yoni as he looked through them. "Did you win or buy them?"

"I bought some to start with," said Yosef, his spirits reviving as he remembered his success with baseball card collecting, "and I won the rest. Want to flip now?"

"Just let me take a look," said Yoni, glancing through the cards to see if he could find some familiar players. "Hey, here's J.R. Richard the Pitcher! Who could forget him?"

"He's not so great," commented Yosef. "He only had one no-hitter, and his batting average is only 231."

"Yeah, I remember some of these guys," said Yoni, lost in his own thoughts. "Here's third baseman, Al Kahn, the catcher, Steve Sladbadnik, the infielder, and RABBEINU ELIAHU, the Gaon of Vilna? What's *he* doing here?"

"Oh," said Yosef, "that's one of my rabbi cards."

"Rabbi cards?"

"Uh huh," Yosef explained. "Rabbi cards. My friend, Danny Brodski, went to Israel last summer to visit his cousins in B'nai Brak. In Israel, they don't have baseball cards. They have rabbi cards, and they win them as prizes in class and things like that. So Danny won a lot of them, and he brought some back for me, too. Then we also made some of our own."

"Hmmm!" said Yoni. He continued to flip through the

cards, and he found among the baseball players Rabbi Yisroal Salanter, Rabbi Yosef Caro, Rabbi Yosef Yitzchak Schneersohn of Lubavitch, and the Baal Shem Tov. "Strange teammates!" he said. "I wonder what these rabbis would have said about baseball?"

"They would have liked it," said Yosef confidently. "My rabbi says that baseball and doing a mitzvoh are a lot alike."

"Come on!" Judah interjected.

"No, really," Yosef insisted, "we all have a yetzer hora, a bad urge, which tries to get us not to do mitzvas. So we all have to go 'up to bat' against it, right?"

Judah and Yoni laughed. "Guess so," they admitted.

"Sure," said Yosef enthusiastically. "Now here is a riddle for you: How is the yetzar hora like a batter?"

"Okay, tell us."

"You have to keep striking him till he's out!" Yosef giggled. "And here's another one: Why did the yetzar hora hate the pitcher?"

When his brothers didn't answer, Yosef said, "cause he wouldn't let him get to first base!" His brothers groaned. "Are there more?" "Uh huh," replied Yosef. "Here's a Chanukah baseball joke: What did the umpire say to the potato latka?" When the older brothers couldn't think of an answer, Yosef smirked, "Batter's up!" and broke into more giggles.

"Yech," said Judah. "Anyway, I bet the yetzar hora wouldn't play ball on Shabbos."

"Yeah?" asked Yosef, sensing a new joke. "Why?"

"Cause he'd have to walk!"

"But no one would want him on their team anyway," said Yoni.

"Why?" questioned Yosef.

"Cause he'd steal first base!"

"UHHHHhh!" Yosef groaned. In the fun, he had forgotten his problems, but all he needed was to hear the word "steal," for him to remember the theft that he was already involved with. It was too much. The Taylor chugged up the Diamonds' driveway. Yosef opened the door and ran to the back yard where the sukkah was, even before the car heaved a weary sigh and stopped.

Five

As she heard the car chug up the driveway, Mrs. Diamond sighed. She especially arose early to savor the delicious minutes of the morning, the quiet time when the boys were away at shul. Well, they were back now, and that meant the day would be in full swing. Breakfast was ready. The door opened, and Mrs. Diamond greeted Judah and Yoni. But Yosef was nowhere to be seen.

"Didn't Yosef go with you?" she asked her older sons.

Judah and Yoni turned around, surprised that Yosef was not following along behind them. Soon the sounds of uneven hammering came from the direction of the sukkah. "He's already at it and he hasn't even eaten breakfast yet!" Mrs. Diamond shook her head and went to the back window. "Yosef!" she called, "come in this minute! Your grilled cheese is ready!"

"The kid still eats grilled cheese for breakfast?" asked Judah.

"It's a healthy breakfast!" The boys and their mother laughed. Yosef, however, was still hammering away at the sukkah.

"Why don't you come in now and wait for Judah and Yoni?" Mrs. Diamond called.

"Cause they take *forever!*" Yosef shouted back.

"For the last time — come in Yosef!"

The door slammed. "I'm here, Mom." Perspiration dripped from under his baseball cap as he went to the sink, washed his hands, and sat down at the table.

"Are you too busy to wash your hands properly?"

"I did wash them, Mom."

"Where? Just the palms? Your knuckles are still black! *And* your hands are still dripping! Don't you believe in drying them?"

Yosef shoved back his chair and went again to the sink. Meanwhile the phone rang. Mrs. Diamond answered it.

"Hello! Oh, hello, Sam, how are you? Yes, we are all in the midst of putting up our sukkah, too. My husband? Of course, just a minute please."

"Yosef," said Mrs. Diamond, "will you please call Daddy to the phone? It is Sam, calling from the nursing home. Daddy is lucky to have him as superintendent for the building. I *do* hope that everything is alright."

Mr. Diamond came in and took the phone. "Hello, Sam. Yes. Oh — again? Twice? So it must be one of the workers and not just a visitor as we thought? But which of our employees would do such a thing? We should use what? *Fingerprint* powder?! You sound like a detective story. Really! Well, I guess the best thing to do would be to look into it. You will? Thanks. Good. I'll be in shortly — see you then." Mr. Diamond hung up the phone. "It happened again," he exclaimed to his wife. "Again two of our staff members had money stolen from their purses."

"Stealers in the nursing home?" piped in Yosef.

"You have to be in on everything?" asked Mr. Diamond, affectionately ruffling his son's baseball cap.

"Hey!" giggled Yosef, "leave my baseball cap alone!"

"You *could* take it off," said Mrs. Diamond. "You've been wearing it constantly since your father cut your hair."

"I like my baseball cap," said Yosef. His father had promised him a crew-cut, but it came out a "baldy," and Yosef was *not* going to take off his baseball cap until his hair grew back in. All the kids in the class would make fun of him. "How are you going to catch them?" he asked again, getting back to the subject.

"Enough!" said his father.

"Oh come on, Daddy!"

"Eat your breakfast," said Yosef's father.

"First wash your hands," said Yosef's mother.

"If all 'stealers' had hands like yours, they would leave smudges on everything they touched, and all the police would have to to would be to look for the one with the dirty hands!" smiled Yoni.

"Lay off!" said Yosef. "If you know so much about catching thieves, go out and catch them!" He washed his hands, slumped into his seat, said "hamotzi"* and bit into his grilled cheese. That made *three* thefts, and not one of them solved.

*Blessing for bread.

25

Six

"Yosef, are you going to help us, or are you going to spend all morning eating grilled cheese?"

"Coming, Judah," Yosef answered, gulping down the last bite. He said the grace after meals quickly and ran out.

"It sure was easier last year," said Yosef, looking over the boards and two-by-fours that his brothers had hauled in the night before. "Last year I could put it up all by myself."

"It will be bigger this year," Judah assured him. "We'll just add on these plywood boards, and more canvas, like this," he added stretching some of the canvas over the frame.

"Not like that!" exclaimed Yosef, "It's coming down over here!"

"Just a minute," said Judah, tugging and pulling.

"It's falling down!" exclaimed Yosef.

"Yosef, cool it!"

"Well, you don't know how to do it! We never should have waited till the last minute. We *have* to have it up by tonight. We have to eat all our meals here, for the whole seven days of Sukkos!"

"So we will! Now just hold on over here, Yosef,"

suggested Yoni, as he attempted to stand up another side of the sukkah. "See? We're getting it now. A little more, a little more. . ."

"No good!" Yosef exclaimed as he let go. "The whole front is caving in."

"If you hadn't let go!" Yoni shouted. "Please Yosef, why don't you go inside and help Shoni with the decorations?"

"I was only helping!" insisted Yosef. "Last year," he repeated, "I could have put the whole thing up by myself!"

"The decorations are almost ready," said Shoni, who had overheard the difficulties her brothers were having with the sukkah. "Will you help me?"

She was busily snipping paper cut-outs. "Will you help me tie strings on them, and then help me hang them up?"

"Sure," replied Yosef agreeably. "I'll stand on the ladder and hang up everything you hand to me."

It was not long before the sukkah was assembled. The canvas walls, securely stretched on their frames, stood taut and sturdy, and the new plywood board extenders also stood straight and very fine. Shoni and Yosef hung the cut-outs and added to their decorations, posters, fruit, and paper chains. The entire Diamond family admired the sukkah — it was certainly the largest and most beautiful one they had ever had.

"But where is the s'chach*?" asked Yosef. "We still need leaves and branches to cover the top of the sukkah. And there has to be enough so that there is more shade

*thatch

than light!"

"We're going to get them right now," Judah assured him, motioning for Yoni and Yosef to follow him toward the car.

But *where* are we going to get it?" Yosef wanted to know.

"Edgewood Park," Judah called over his shoulder.

"Did you get permission? If you didn't, then I'm not going!"

"The park commission is allowing people to get s'chach for their sukkah from the area near the swamp. Now come on! It's getting late, as you would say!"

Yosef didn't move. "Come on, Yos, shake a leg," Yoni said, about to follow Judah to the car.

"First, I have to tell you the story my rabbi told us."

"Now? Tell it in the car, okay? What's the matter with you?"

"I have to tell you now. It's important."

"Hey, come on, you guys!" Judah yelled coming back to the yard.

"Yosef has to tell us something," Yoni answered.

"Okay, we're listening," said Judah. "Just make it fast."

"Don't rush me," Yosef said, and then began:

"Once there was this rabbi, I think his name was Rabbi Moses. One day he was traveling by coach to another city. They came to this place where there were rows and rows of apple trees.

"When the coachman saw the trees, he became very excited. 'Are we lucky!' he shouted to the rabbi. 'Look at this orchard! These apples are fit for a king! In fact, they *do* belong to the king. This is the king's royal orchard. But I still have an idea how we can get some apples. I'll go into the orchard, and you be the lookout. If you see anybody coming, you just yell.'

"The rabbi didn't want to do it. He knew it would be stealing. So he thought of a plan, and said. 'Alright, I'll stand watch.' The coachman ran quickly across the road, and began climbing the fence. Just as he reached the top, the rabbi called out, 'He's watching! He sees us'

"As soon as he heard that, the coachman leaped from the fence, dashed for the coach, and whipped the horses to speed away as fast as they could. As the coach bounced down the road, the coachman kept looking back to see if anyone was chasing them. But he didn't see anyone, so he finally slowed down a bit. 'Whew! Am I lucky!' he gasped, as he wiped his forehead. 'Thanks a lot for letting me know. By the way, who was it? Did one of the royal guards come out? Or was it just an ordinary watchman?'

"The rabbi shook his head. 'Not the watchman, *or* the guards,' he said, 'It was the King himself.'

" 'The *King?*' gasped the coachman. 'How could it be?'

" 'I mean the King of all Kings, the Ruler of the whole world. G-d Himself was watching,' Rabbi Moses answered."

As he finished telling the story, Yosef took a deep

breath and looked at his brothers.

"Stop worrying, Yosef," Judah said smiling, "Rabbi Mendles arranged it all with the Park Commission. Shabbos morning he announced that we all have permission to take the s'chach that we need. We wouldn't go otherwise."

Seven

The Taylor chugged carefully along the narrow dirt road that lead to the Edgewood Park swamp. The road was muddy from the rain of a week ago, and it also had a lot of pits. The car's tires squelched through the mud, hobbled over the holes and finally just sighed and stopped. "We need a storm-trooper, not a Taylor," joked Yoni.

Judah wasn't so pleased. "You won't think it so 'punny' when we have to carry the 's'chach' all the way up here from the swamp," he said.

Where's the swamp?" Yosef wanted to know.

"I *think* it's just around the next curve and down a little hill," said Judah. "Let's get the sickle and shears, and we'll go and leave the car here. We'll have to carry back the s'chach. Then, I *think* we'll be able to back the car out. At least I *hope* so."

The boys got out of the car. Yosef was not happy about these developments. He did not like the fact that their car was stuck on a lonely, narrow road, where there was not even room to turn around, and he did not like the fact that they would have to carry the s'chach this extra distance, which would also take plenty of time. It was already getting late. Maybe they wouldn't even be back before evening! He had his own reasons for wanting to get back early, but now maybe they wouldn't even get back at all! There seemed to be nobody here in the park besides them. Everyone else must have gotten their s'chach earlier in the day. A few birds tittered, and a crow cawed. Yosef remembered that there was probably also a 'loose thief' somewhere in the area, and here they were, alone in some deserted swampy place, just like where a thief would want to escape to. The crow cawed again.

"Let's get out of here," said Yosef. "Let's go home."

"Oh come on, Yosef, we have to get the s'chach."

"Don't we have some bamboo poles from last year that we can use?"

"There aren't enough. Remember, the sukkah is bigger now. Don't worry about our getting out. We aren't stuck really. The road is just too narrow and overgrown for us to go on. Come on. Let's get the shears and sickles. We'll just cut down the reeds and go right home."

Yosef, reluctantly, followed his older brothers. However, when he saw the gracefully curved sickles, with their razor-sharp edges, his mood changed.

"I want to use one of the sickles."

"But it is almost as big as you are," said Judah. "Besides, you don't even know how it works."

"Oh yes I do."

"There's not time!"

"Oh come on, Judah! I can do it."

"For you we brought hedge shears," said Judah sternly.

Yosef persisted, insisting to use the sickle until they reached the bottom of the hill, where the swamp — wasn't.

"What do we do now?" asked Judah.

"Let's go back to the road," suggested Yoni. "I think there's a clearing a little further on."

The boys returned to the road, and walked a little more slowly now, carrying their weighty equipment.

"What was that?" said Yosef suddenly.

His two brothers started. "It's nothing!" said Judah, at last. "Probably a squirrel."

"No!" Yosef insisted. "I know someone is following us — and what if it's that escaped thief?"

"That's crazy, Yos," said Yoni, a little uneasy.

The boys continued, slowly, cautiously.

"Someone is coming!" whispered Yosef hoarsely.

"Chipmunks," Judah insisted, but the boys stopped walking. There *were* footsteps.

"Stop right where you are!"

The boys turned. There was a man coming out of the woods!

Eight

"You touch me or my brothers and I'll *shear* you!"
Yosef wanted to say, but the words stuck in his throat, and
his hands froze to his sides.

"It's the park commissioner," said Judah, somewhat
embarrassed by his own relief, as he recognized the neat
brown uniform.

"He's wearing tzitzis!" exclaimed Yoni.

The park commissioner laughed as he held up his
tzitzis, and the boys smiled also, as they held up theirs.

"Park Commissioner Elyon, at your service," the park
commissioner said. "And you young men must be here to
collect s'chach."

The boys nodded, too surprised to see a park commissioner with tzitzis, to reply.

"I just wanted to tell you," said the park commissioner,
"that you are in the wrong place — which you must have
figured out for yourselves by now. You should have gone
left when the road forked, a little while back. That would
take you to the swamp. This area here is the nature
reserve. Visitors don't usually come this way. Hmmm,"
he added, admiringly. "Look at those sickles. I haven't
seen any like that for a long time. How about if I come

along with you and thresh a few reeds myself?"

Needless to say, the boys were happy to have his company. When all were in the car, it zoomed easily backwards down the road, and when they came to the fork, Judah shifted into forward gear. The Taylor then resumed its usual chug.

"I've never seen a car that races backwards with such ease, and yet plods forward with such difficulty," commented the Park Commissioner.

"It's easy to rip out stitches, but it takes time to sew them," explained Yoni.

"I don't understand. . ." began Mr. Elyon.

"Our car is a Taylor!" blurted out Yoni, as Yosef burst into hysterical giggles, and even Judah smiled.

Mr. Elyon looked around. "What do you know!" he exclaimed. "I haven't seen one since my boyhood! And the sickles really look old — almost like archeological finds. Where did you get them?"

"We just had them in the family," Judah explained.

"Maybe, when things are used to do mitzvahs, they last a long time," suggested Mr. Elyon. "Here's the swamp."

It took only a few minutes to thresh all the reeds that the Diamonds could possibly use. Judah had thought that *he* knew how to swing a sickle, but Mr. Elyon swung the curved blade so deftly, he looked like he had been doing it all his life.

"I almost *have*," Mr. Elyon admitted. "When I was going to school, I used to cut down s'chach and sell it to earn some money!"

After the reeds were cut, the boys gathered them by armloads and carried them to the Taylor to load them in bundles on the car's roof carrier. When the reeds were securely tied down, Judah checked his watch. It seemed amazing, but with Mr. Elyon's help, they were actually ahead of schedule.

"Can we give you a ride anywhere?" he asked Mr. Elyon.

Mr. Elyon looked at the sun. "Almost three," he said. "I *would* appreciate a ride home. We just moved to Crescent Drive. Would that be out of your way?"

"Not at all," said Judah, as they all climbed into the car once again.

"You just moved into town?" asked Yoni as the car began to chug along.

Mr. Elyon nodded. "We came just after Yom Kipper."

"It's a good thing that you *did* come!" piped in Yosef. "You know, even right now, probably, there is a *thief* running around loose here somewhere!"

"Aw, come on, Yos," Yoni hushed him.

"No, the boy is right," said the park commissioner, "except for one thing."

"What's that?" questioned Yosef eagerly.

"There *was* a thief running around loose here. But we caught him in the park — this morning!"

"You *caught* him!" exclaimed Yosef.

"In Edgewood Park?" exclaimed Yoni.

"Sounds like a detective story," said Judah, shaking his head as he continued to steer the Taylor straight along the road.

"I hardly expected it myself," admitted Park Commissioner Elyon. "When I heard that the thief had escaped, I thought he would be far away from here by now. Still, I had his description, and a description of his car. And then, of course, I remembered learning the Gemora*, which teaches us how Rabbi Elazar, the son of Shimon Bar Yochai, used to catch thieves."

"How was that?" Yosef wanted to know.

"He would go to the inns, where people used to come for food and drink. He would go in the middle of the morning, when most people were up and going about their work. A few people would be having breakfast. If he found anyone falling asleep over their eggs and cereal, he would suspect that they were a thief. Because is someone is sleeping during the day, then they were probably up during the night. And thieves, of course, *do* work at night."

"Of course," continued the park commissioner, "not everyone who sleeps during the day, is a thief. Still, if I see someone in the park sleeping during the day, I take a second look to see who they are. *This* particular person fit the description of the thief, and his car fit the description of the get-away car. So we arrested him and sent him back to prison. And now, the area is safe."

"Wow," sighed Yosef. Look at that, he thought to

*Portions of oral law written down.

himself. The Gemora showed the park commissioner how to arrest a runaway prisoner. I wonder what it says about arresting people who steal baseball cards? I've got to find a solution and I'm in a real pickle till I do.

"That's some story," said Judah and Yoni appreciatively.

"If you just moved here, you probably haven't even had time to put up your own sukkah," began Yoni.

"Our house has a little porch," replied Mr. Elyon, "so we did put up a little sukkah. But the people of this community are so nice, that they all want to welcome us. They are insisting that we come to eat with them in their sukkahs, so I don't know how much use we will get out of our little one. In fact, tonight we are invited to join a family by the name of Diamond. Do you boys know them?"

"Know them?" exclaimed the brothers. "We *are* them!"

"That just proves that nice parents have nice children!" smiled Mr. Elyon. "Mrs. Diamond mentioned to my wife that she had a son the same age as our Benji. That must be you," said Mr. Elyon to Yosef.

Yosef grinned, "Mom said that there would be some boys my age who were coming. Also a boy named Ted Winters is coming, but I don't think his parents are."

Mr. Elyon nodded. "We certainly are looking forward to joining you," he said as they pulled into the driveway to his house. "And thank you boys again for driving me home."

"Thank you!" called the boys. The Taylor zoomed

backwards down the driveway, and then resumed its usual chug-along pace.

"What time is it?" asked Yosef.

"Almost two-twenty," replied Yoni.

Yosef was nervous. "Let's hurry and finish the sukkah," he urged. "You know, tonight is also erev Shabbos.* Shabbos and Sukkos! So we have to be ready even earlier!"

"We're going as fast as we can," said Judah.

When the boys reached home, Judah and Yoni wanted to rest for awhile, but Yosef wouldn't hear of it. He quickly climbed the ladder to spread the s'chach on the roof of the sukkah. That finished, the only thing left to be done was to put in the table and chairs. Which table? They had a little folding table, but when they used it last year there was no elbow room. Now that the sukkah was bigger, there would probably be room for the round redwood picnic table from the yard. Yosef eyed the picnic table. It would be perfect. It wouldn't be hard to move either. He would be able to turn it on its side and roll it. As he was turning the table over, Judah and Yoni came out from their juice and cookies break.

"What are you doing?" exclaimed Judah.

"It will never fit through the door," warned Yoni.

"It would take up too much room anyway," reasoned Judah. "We won't be able to get in or out of the sukkah."

"No, it *is* going to fit," Yosef stubbornly assured them. "We want to be comfortable when we eat our meals, don't

*Sabbath eve.

we? Just watch. It will fit. You'll see."

Judah and Yoni were too tired to argue. They watched as Yosef struggled to ease the large table through the sukkah door. If fit — to a hair's breadth.

"Now what time is it?" asked Yosef as he proudly surveyed the table and chairs, fit for a king.

"Just three," yawned Yoni.

"Great!" exclaimed Yosef enthusiastically. "I knew if I hurried, it would pay off. We don't light Shabbos candles until six-thirty, — which gives you three and a half hours to nap! See? I want to pay you back for the sleep that I stole from you this morning. A nap now is better than nothing, isn't it?"

Judah and Yoni looked at each other. "Better than nothing?" asked Yoni, "I don't know what could beat it!"

He and Judah went inside, leaving Yosef to admire the sukkah, and to go over in his mind the day's accomplishments. The sukkah was put up on time. The Edgewood Park thief was caught, and his own theft of time was paid back the best he could. Unsolved problems still to be faced, were the theft of the baseball cards, the theft at his father's office, and also, well, it wasn't exactly a problem, but was still something new to face, and that was the two new boys who were joining them for dinner. Yosef wondered what they would be like.

Nine

The boys seemed shy, that was for sure. Benji was new in town, and Ted, although he had lived in the area for a while, had never eaten in a sukkah. Ted looked around, obviously not knowing what anything was for, but he was too embarrassed to ask any questions. Everything was new for him — the eating outside in the drafty sukkah on the cool October night, the washing "al natilas yadayim" by pouring water over his hands with the strange cup with the two handles on it, then not saying anything until Yosef's father said "Hamotzi" — and *then* eating the slice of round delicious challah, which was first dipped in honey. The grownups were doing a lot of talking, but the other boys his age who were there, hardly said anything at all. Now they were eating the gefilte fish which wasn't from a can, either. Mrs. Diamond must have made it, and it really was good. He had met Mrs. Diamond when he was substituting on the paper route here. She was a nice lady. She always smiled at him and said hello, and asked how he was. A few of the other people on the route did that too, but then one day she asked him if he was Jewish. He said yes, and then she asked him is he would like to join them for a meal in their sukkah. So he said yes, but that was mostly because he was too embarrassed to say no. How could he say no when she asked to nicely? She made it seem that they would not be able to enjoy their holiday at all unless he came and enjoyed it too. That was a crazy idea, he thought when he got home, and he really did not plan on coming tonight. Except that Mrs. Diamond somehow got hold of his phone number, and she called him this afternoon to remind him, please, wouldn't he come. He couldn't get out of it. So he came, but now that he was here, everything was so strange that he wasn't sure visiting in the Diamond sukkah was such a good idea.

"Yosef, can you help me in the kitchen, please?"

When Yosef went outside the sukkah, he was pretty sure that his mother wanted him for something besides serving the soup.

"While Daddy is talking with Mr. Elyon, won't you please do something to make the boys feel at home?"

"I don't know what to *say,* Mom!" Yosef was not unfriendly, but he could be shy.

"I'm sure you can think of something," encouraged Mrs. Diamond. "They are very nice boys. They are waiting for you to 'break the ice.' "

Yosef thought for a minute, and decided that when he went back to the sukkah he would tell some "nonsense riddles." With all the decorations hanging in the sukkah, they would be able to think of a lot of "punny" things. He was right, for the other boys caught on right away, and soon they were giggling and cackling endlessly.

"What did one apple say to the other?" Yosef began. No one got it, so he smirked, "We aren't a pear!"

"Which fruit conquered Rome?" ventured Ted. "Alexander the Grape!"

"Which fruit has the hardest hands?" asked Benji. "The pomegranate!"

"What did one banana say to the other?" "You're appealing!"

"What did the dates say when they agreed to go out to lunch?" "It's a date!"

"What did the mother olive say to her children?" "Olive you!"

That was only warm-ups, for then with some help from Judah, Yoni and Shoni they began with the "parsha puns."

"Who was the greatest actor in the Bible?" quipped Yoni.

"Samson!" giggled Yosef. "He brought down the house!"

"When did Moses sleep five in a bed?" asked Shoni.

Yosef remembered that one too: "When he slept with his forefathers."

Benji Elyon got the idea, "Who was Jonah's teacher?" he asked. No one knew. "The whale that brought him up!"

Everyone groaned. "Who was the straightest man in the Bible?" asked Yosef. Everyone seemed to know: "Joseph, because Pharaoh made a ruler out of him!"

Yosef gave a wide smile, and bowed, as though he was

that Joseph.

"What time of day was Adam created?" asked Shoni. "Just a little before Eve."

Ted remembered a joke he had heard: "Where did Noah strike the first nail in the ark?" No one had heard it before. Ted felt pretty good, and smiled "right on the head!" Everyone laughed.

"Where was tennis mentioned in the Bible?" asked Yoni. "When Yosef served in Pharaoh's court!"

Yosef bowed, and countered, "Why did Adam bite the apple Eve gave him?"

"Cause he didn't have a knife!" exclaimed Benji. "Which animal took the most luggage into the ark?"

"It must have been the elephant," replied Ted, "cause he had to take his trunk!" Everyone roared.

"Enough" Mr. Diamond interrupted at last. "Okay, boys, you've had you little warmup. I must say your riddles are "berry punny." But now let's see if you can answer a few riddles that I have for you. Are you ready?" The boys nodded and waited. On Friday night and holidays, Yosef's father and the other members of the family had riddles to ask on Torah subjects, and someone always shared a story from the Torah that they had learned that week.

Questions and answers went back and forth, but Ted already had a lot to think about. All his teachers said that he had a "good head," and he liked subjects like math and electronics. But at home he could just not imagine his whole family sitting around the dinner table and getting so excited about fractions and multiplication tables, or about electric circuits and magnetic fields. Yet Yosef was his age, and look how excited all the Diamonds were about the things that Yosef was learning in school. Yosef, his older brothers and sister, his father and mother — they all seemed to be interested in learning the same things. Sunday school stories?

Well, *he* had always thought so. He had always thought that the things he learned in the Sunday "religious education program" were just stories. But Yosef and his family were talking about the sukkahs that *"we"* built when *"we"* were freed from Egypt as though it *really* happened — to *them!* Well, that was another riddle, how they could have been there when it happened so long ago. But they sure seemed to know what they were talking about — and having fun together, too. Ted had never seen *his* family have so much fun together. That was another thing that he thought happened only in books. Ted decided that he would do some investigation.

"Yosef! Put those away and eat your chicken!" Mr. Diamond's stern voice interrupted Ted's thoughts. Ted looked up just in time to catch a glimpse of Yosef tossing five little lead cubes up from the back of his hand, and catching them all again in one swipe. "My kugelach," Yosef grinned in explanation. "They're like jacks, only without a ball. They play them in Israel." Yosef, who had been practicing kugelach for weeks, at breakfast, lunch, dinner, and in-between, had become a master at the game. "Don't worry," Yosef assured his new friends, "we can all play with them after dessert."

Dessert was honey cake, dessert whip, and hot fudge sauce, which was delicious, just as all of the meal had been.

"You sure are a great cook, Mrs. Diamond," said Ted appreciatively.

Mrs. Diamond smiled, "It's because of that special ingredient: Shabbos!"

"And Sukkos," added Yosef.

Before Ted knew what was happening, little books were passed out so everyone could say a special prayer after eating, which they called "bentching." The bentching was written in little print, Hebrew on one side of the page, and English on the other. Ted read the English the best he could in the shadowy sukkah light.

Immediately after "bentching," Yosef brought out the "kugelach." He really knew how to throw them up in the air and catch them. Ted and Benji kept trying, but they couldn't get the hang of it.

"Here, let me show you again," said Yosef, concentrating on all the routines. "You want to try again?"

"No, thanks," answered Benji and Ted, putting up their hands, admitting Yosef's mastery of the game.

"Tell me what school you go to," asked Ted.

"I haven't gone there yet," replied Benji, "because we just moved here. But I will be going to the one that Yosef goes to, the Talmud Torah."

"I've heard of it," said Ted. "But I thought it was only for religious kids."

Yosef shrugged. "It's a good school. I like it. My brothers went there too."

"Well, I probably couldn't go there anyways," said Ted. "I don't know all that stuff you've been learning up until now. I'd be way behind. Besides, I bet it costs a lot of money."

"No way," said Yosef. "Everyone goes who wants to. There's a scholarship fund. And we have lots of guys who come in and catch up. They learn with tutors. It's not hard. One guy came in last year and he didn't even know the Hebrew alphabet. Now he's one of the best in the class."

"Well, *I* already know the Hebrew alphabet," said Ted.

"See?" said Yosef. "And we have real good baseball teams, too. Do you like to play infield?"

The rest of the evening centered around baseball talk. Of course, Yosef pulled out his baseball cards, and his new friends admired his collection.

"I've got a collection too," said Ted. "Sometime we'll have to flip."

The clock above the Diamonds' mantle piece chimed ten o'clock.

"So late?" exclaimed Ted. "I better go. I told my Mom I'd be home by now."

"Come back soon!" Yosef said, walking him to the

door.

"I hope he does come to the Talmud Torah," said Benji, as Yosef came back into the living room.

"Yeah, me too," said Yosef, a little sleepily.

Soon it was time for Benji and his parents to leave. After Yosef's parents said goodnight to them, Mrs. Diamond came back to the living room.

"Wall-to-wall baseball cards!" she commented. "Yosef, I'm glad you and the other boys enjoyed yourself. I knew that you would find a way to break the ice with them."

Yosef didn't answer.

"You all had a good time, didn't you?" Mrs. Diamond repeated.

"—What, Mom?"

"Didn't you hear me? I guess you must be tired after a long day. We're getting up early tomorrow to go to shul, so why don't you pick up these baseball cards and get some sleep?"

Baseball cards were not exactly what Yosef wanted to hear about. It hadn't bothered him while the other boys were here, while they had been joking and having fun together, but now that he was alone and the house was quiet, all the ball players seemed to look like David, Ari or Michael.

"Yosef? Aren't you going to put them away?"

"—What? Yeah, Mom, I am. Right now."

Maybe tonight David and Ari were also looking

through their baseball cards — their *stolen* cards. How could they eat peaceably in their sukkah with stolen baseball cards? And how could *he,* Yosef, eat peaceably in *his* sukkah *knowing* that they stole the baseball cards, and that they were getting away with it? They were, too, because if he didn't say anything, nobody would ever know.

So what if no one ever knew? How many baseball cards could it have been anyway? Maybe ten packs. So Michael's father might get upset at first, but probably he would buy Michael ten more packs of baseball cards. Then what difference would it make? Michael would have baseball cards, and everyone would forget the whole thing. Right?

Yosef slowly picked up his baseball cards. "Wrong," said Steve Platter, the infielder. "Wrong," said "Bugs" Susby, the catcher. "No way," grinned Flip Gireson, third baseman.

"Okay," thought Yosef. "Right, I'm wrong. I wouldn't forget. And David and Ari won't forget either. They'll always have it in for me, knowing I could snitch on them. Even if I don't, they'll treat me as if I could and would. And that is just as bad."

"Besides," Yosef continued to think, "if they could steal Michael's baseball cards, then they could steal other baseball cards too. And they might not even stop at baseball cards. They could steal anything. And they would always know that I knew that they did it. It would get worse and worse. I've got to stop them, now. But how?"

Yosef looked at the players, but they had no solutions. It was late. Tomorrow, they would go to shul. They would come home and eat in the sukkah. The next day, Sunday, was still Sukkos, so he wouldn't have to face them in school until Monday. That was a long time off. Yosef put the rest of the cards in the cigar box. Before Monday there was time to think of a lot of answers — at least he *hoped* so!

Ten

Sun streamed in through Yosef's window. It was a completely perfect day. "Mode Ani Lifonecha!" he began to sing. "I give thanks to You, G-d, for returning my soul to me!" Yes, he said that every morning, but today he was going to make himself *feel* it. Sukkos was, after all, the "festival of our rejoicing," and Yosef had had in mind that this Sukkos he really *was* going to rejoice. He had not forgotten about the baseball cards dilemma, but why should a few stolen baseball cards ruin his rejoicing on Sukkos? Besides, if he really rejoiced, then G-d might help him think of what to do about the baseball cards. "Happy Sukkos!" he called to Judah, who was not exactly up yet. "It *is* time to get up," he urged the still dozing household. "Happy Sukkos, Yoni! Good Shabbos, and *Happy* Sukkos!"

In time, the rest of the Diamond family were up, dressed and on their way to shul. "What a lovely day," commented Mrs. Diamond as they began to walk toward the shul. "They say it is a good 'simmon,' a good sign, for the rest of the year if the weather is pleasant on Sukkos."

"This dog seems to like it too!" grinned Yosef, pointing to a shaggy-haired brown and white dog who had started to follow them. "Good Shabbos, good Shabbos!" Yosef said to the dog. The dog wagged his tail, and continued on its way. "I always say Good Shabbos and then the dogs leave me alone," Yosef explained. "Why don't you try it, Shoni," he added, turning to his sister, "and then you won't be afraid."

"They don't follow *me,*" Shoni retorted. "They follow *you* because you are singing in the street. Mom, would you please tell him to stop singing? He can sing in shul."

"I know that I can sing in shul," Yosef responded, "but I want to practice the 'Anim Zmiros' prayer just in case they let me go up to lead it."

"You know Yosef loves to sing, Shoni," said Mrs. Diamond. "We are the only ones on the street, now. I don't think anyone can hear him."

Shoni knew, but she couldn't help feeling embarrassed. Rejoicing on Sukkos was one thing, but singing in the street was something else. "Look Mom," said Shoni in a low voice, "Here is Mrs. Morgenstern coming out of her house right now. Please tell Yosef to be quiet, okay?"

At shul Yosef tried to concentrate, but it was very hard, and his mind kept wandering back to baseball cards. "Hey, what happened to my rejoicing?" he asked himself, shaking his head, trying to loosen intruding thoughts from his mind. Yoni nudged him, *"What* are you doing?" "Dovening!"* Yosef hissed back. He tried to immerse himself in the blessings. He remembered his rabbi telling the class that the reason G-d gives you difficult situations

*praying

is to test you. "Am I passing?" Yosef thought to himself. "That the baseball cards were stolen is a hard enough test, but that I have to forget about it to doven is even harder." Yosef had a vision in his mind. Again he saw David and Ari bending over the stolen packs. But this time, he, Yosef, quickly got all the other kids in the class to come and see. Without a peep, all the other kids in the class tiptoe in to the classroom and witness, unseen, the two boys sorting the cards. Finally, David and Ari must be getting a tingling feeling on their backs, because they turn around. And everyone, *everyone* points a finger at them! "Aaahhhh!"

Again he shook his head, very hard, and plunged into his dovening, giving it all he had.

The kiddush at shul was beautiful. The shul sukkah was decorated with all kinds of fruit, especially those from the land of Israel: grapes, dates, figs, and pomegranate. On the wall opposite the entrance was a beautiful embroidered cloth which one of the women had made. Embroidered all around the cloth were fruits, and within that was a caravan of people, marching all around the cloth, to represent the Jews bringing their first fruits to Jerusalem, as they did every Sukkos in the days when the holy Temple was still standing. In the center of the cloth was embroidered, in purple and gold thread, the names of all the ushpizin: guests who come to the sukkah, Avraham, Isaac, Jacob, Joseph, Moshe, Aharon, and David. Shoni and her mother went up to the cloth to admire its intricate artistry,

54

and to praise the skill and patience of the woman who had embroidered it. Yosef looked at it also, but his mind was on something else.

"Each night all of the Ushpizin come to the sukkah," he thought. "And each night a different one of them leads. Tonight the leader is our father Abraham."

When *he* was a boy, he wasn't afraid to tell the truth. Everyone he knew, even his own family bowed down to idols, but *he* didn't. He told everyone, even King Nimrod, that there was only One G-d, and that the idols were only stone and wood. He wasn't afraid of anything. *He* told the truth.

The rabbi was making kiddush now, and everyone was passing around tiny plastic cups of wine and big pieces of cake. "Here, Yosef," said Shoni, passing him wine and the chocolate marble cake that he usually liked. "Thanks, Shoni," Yosef replied absently. He wasn't even hungry.

"What's the matter with you?" asked his sister. "You don't feel good?"

"I'm all right, okay?" said Yosef. He sounded angry, and Shoni didn't want to start an argument right in the middle of the sukkah. She left him the cake and went to talk to her friends.

Well, he wasn't hungry, but after all, it *was* cake, so he ate it. He glanced around and saw that someone was trying to open the door of the sukkah, but the door was stuck. The sukkah was very crowded. Yosef nudged through the people and pushed the door open. It was Ted.

"Hi," said Ted a little shyly. "I wanted to come, but I guess I'm a little late."

"Oh, don't worry about it," said Yosef. "Some other people also got to the sukkah late, and they are making kiddush now. So you can listen to them, and then have some cake."

Ted nodded and he and Yosef edged over to where they could hear the kiddush. Yosef got a little cup of the kiddush wine for Ted, and then offered him cake, which he took gratefully. He hadn't known exactly where the shul was, and he had gotten lost on the way. He had almost given up and gone home, but then someone gave him good directions. Even then he almost didn't go, because he was pretty sure he would be too late. "What's the use of going when everyone will probably be gone already?" he had thought. But he was curious to see the sukkah of the shul. Yosef had mentioned that it was even bigger than the one that the Diamonds' had in their back yard.

"Hey, this really is a big sukkah," said Ted, admiring the sturdy wooden walls, which were panelled. "It's almost nice enough to live in all year round, except for the grass roof!"

"Corn stalks," Yosef giggled. "It's nice for a nice day, but when it rains you get cornstalks dripping all over you!"

All of a sudden everything seemed funny. Yosef stopped worrying about the baseball cards, and Ted no longer felt awkward that he came late. There was a little more room in the sukkah now, because some of the people had left, so they helped themselves to more cake and soda, and giggled together.

"What's so funny?" asked Yoni.

"Cornstalks!" blurted out Yosef.

"I don't get it," said Yoni, "but anyway, glad to see you, Ted. You'll come back with us, right?"

Ted nodded, happily. He was glad he hadn't gone back home, glad he hadn't given up.

Some of the men were beginning to sing songs now, but they weren't songs Ted knew. Ted listened. The songs weren't words. They were feelings — his own feelings too — and the feelings came out in a melody. Simple melodies. Some of the men were stamping their feet and clapping their hands — then some men put their hands on each other's shoulders and began dancing. A little boy joined in and his father lifted him on his shoulders and they danced together. Now Yoni was dancing too, and Judah and Mr. Diamond. "Yosef!" called Yoni.

Mrs. Diamond came over to the boys. "Good to see you, Ted," she greeted. "Aren't you boys going to join the dancing?"

Ted smiled, a little embarrassed. It didn't look like it was hard to "dance" like the men. There weren't any fancy steps — they were just going in a circle to the music. But Yosef seemed shy.

"Aw, Mom," Yosef began. Sometimes, when he was in the mood, he would begin dancing almost before anyone else. But today... Ted wouldn't join in unless he did. Then

Yosef shook his head. He wasn't going to be a party pooper on Sukkos. "Let's go!" he shouted to Ted.

So the two boys joined the circle. Soon someone pulled them in to a little circle in the center of the other circle, and Yosef, more in the swing of it now, began to do Russian leg-kicks. Ted, who was pretty good at this himself, began to do the same. The two boys smiled at each other, and without even discussing anything, began to work out a routine together. First they kicked in time together, and then Yosef got up and began to jump over Ted as he was kicking, the then Ted began to jump over Yosef while Yosef was kicking. Then Yosef tried to kick with a paper cup on his nose. It soon fell off, but Ted grabbed it before it hit the floor, and soon the boys were tossing the paper cup back and forth while they were kicking, until everyone was exhausted.

"Not bad!" exclaimed Yosef, as he and Ted sat on the floor together.

"Beats football practice," panted Ted. "Betcha I'll be sore tomorrow!"

The boys laughed, and Mrs. Diamond called, "come on, you Russian dancers! It's time to go home for lunch."

That night Yosef lay in bed, with Sukkos scenes flashing through his mind. Ted had joined them for all the meals. These two days he and Yosef had become pretty good friends. Tomorrow, though, was *Chol HaMoed Sukkos,* the intermediate days, and there would be school. Ted had said he would like to go to Yosef's school.

Too bad he won't start tomorrow, so that Yosef wouldn't have to face David and Ari alone.

"I know what I'll do," Yosef thought to himself. "I'll say I have to use the bathroom during class, and then I'll take the stolen cards out of David's locker, and give them back to Michael. But no, that's not a good idea, because they'll know it was me who gave them back, and then they'll get me. They know I saw they were keeping them in the locker. I bet it was David's idea. Ari does anything that David says. Makes David feel like a big shot. So what am I going to do? I want to help Michael, but I don't want them to gang up on me. If only I could think of something." And tossing and turning Yosef finally fell asleep.

When Yosef awoke the next morning, there was no magic answer in his head. He got up, dressed himself, and prepared his books and school supplies. His parents were already downstairs having breakfast.

"Ruth," Yosef's father was saying, "have you noticed that Yosef has not been his usual self? He barely seems to hear when someone talks to him. It used to be we couldn't get a word in edgewise, but now I have to pull words out of him. I wonder what's wrong with him?"

"I've noticed it too," replied his mother, "but I think it may be just a growing stage. It's probably nothing," she said as she began clearing off the table.

"He's taking a long time this morning too" Mr. Diamond observed. "I wonder what's taking him so long? He's usually the first one down here. I have to leave for the office early. I have a meeting this morning with Sam, to see what we can do about those pocketbook thefts at the office. I'll let you know what happens tonight."

"Good luck, dear," said Mrs. Diamond, just as Yosef came down the steps. "I'll eat something in school, Mom," he greeted her before she could insist that he eat breakfast. "If I don't get a ride with Dad, I'll be late."

At school, Yosef couldn't concentrate.

"According to Jewish Law," Rabbi Golder was saying, "a thief who steals at night, gets a harsher sentence than an armed robber who robs by day."

"Yosef?" warned Rabbi Golder. "Why aren't you paying attention? Can you tell the class why this is so?"

Out of the corner of his eye, Yosef saw David and Ari laugh. He tried to concentrate, but couldn't.

"Uh, uh" he said, as if he didn't know. He actually knew it cold, but he couldn't get the words out of his mouth. Rabbi Golder called on Josh.

"A thief," Josh explained, "steals in the night when people can't see him. But an armed robber steals by day, when he can be seen.

"An armed robber, who steals by day, shows that he is afraid neither of man nor of G-d. But the thief, who steals only at night, is given a worse punishment, because he is more afraid of man than of G-d."

"Thank you for answering the question." said Rabbi Golder. Yosef slumped in his seat. He couldn't wait until class was over. He had a problem, and he couldn't concentrate on anything else. These past few days, he had tried to put it out of his mind but he couldn't do that any longer.

When he got home, things weren't much better. "Yosef, you haven't touched the spaghetti," his mother said. "Are you feeling alright? You love spaghetti."

"Every food is his favorite food," piped in Shoni.

"Well, at least I like foods and eat, not like you. You only like gum, candy, soda, popcorn, potato chips, pretzels, and all the other junk food," Yosef snapped back.

"Wait a minute," his mother interrupted. "Yosef, calm down and Shoni, your comment wasn't necessary or nice."

"Well, I didn't really mean anything by it or expect him to get so huffy. It was only a joke," Shoni explained.

"She's always picking on me," Yosef said, running out of the room.

"What's wrong, Yos?" Yoni asked, following after him, "You're so touchy lately."

"Nothing Yoni, and stop laughing at me!"

"I wasn't laughing," said Yoni, trying to put on a serious face. Yoni thought everything he did was funny, thought Yosef. Just because I'm younger. According to Yoni, you have to be seventeen before you can have a serious problem!

So Yosef went to his room and didn't say anything. He had hardly eaten anything all day, but he wasn't even hungry. He just didn't know what to do.

Even just *being* in school was awful. Ari and David were looking at him all the time, and between classes they would find ways to "accidentally" bump into him, and hiss in his ear "You better keep your mouth shut, or else!" If only *he* could go to another school! But deep down he knew that wasn't really an answer. There was probably a David and Ari in every school. But what could he do?

"Are you still up, Yosef?" said his mother. "Usually you're asleep the minute your head touches the pillow. What's wrong?"

"Oh, nothing, nothing," Yosef mumbled.

"Then say Shma, the bedtime prayer, and you'll fall asleep," she said, turning off Yosef's light and closing the door behind her.

Yosef lay awake in the dark. He saw himself in school, standing in line waiting for a drink of water. Suddenly someone bumped into his left shoulder, and almost knocked him down. "You tell and we'll getcha!" hissed David. He saw himself back in class, learning Chumash, suddenly a fist-sized paper wad smashed against the back of his head, "Don't tell!" snarled Ari from behind him. Later, after school, Yosef was walking down the steps when, before he knew it, he stumbled and was falling down and down and down. He was about to crash into the sidewalk, but before he did, he saw chalked on the pavement: "Open you mouth and we'll get you!!" Yosef woke up trembling. At school it was bad enough, but now they were in his dreams too!

"Yosef?" said his mother when she heard he youngest son knocking at the door. "What's the matter? Why are you still up?"

Yosef came in and shook his head.

"Did you have a bad dream?" his mother asked kindly. It was too much. Yosef couldn't hold back the tears anymore, and before he knew it he was trembling all over.

"I'm so scared," he sobbed. "But I can't tell you."

"Can't tell me what?" asked Mrs. Diamond, wondering what could have put her son in such a cold sweat.

"You promise you won't tell?" Yosef was still trembling.

"I promise," Mrs. Diamond assured him. "And whatever it is, you'll feel better getting it off your chest. And I'll try to help if I can," she added, holding him close to her. By this time Yosef's father was up, too.

"Hey, I have to get some sleep tonight!" he mumbled. But when he saw Yosef's face he said, "What is it, Yosef? What's the matter?"

So Yosef blurted out the entire story. How he caught David and Ari with the baseball cards. How they had threatened him. How he couldn't think what to do about it, and how they kept threatening him, worse and worse it seemed, every day.

When he finished, at first his parents didn't say anything. "I know how you feel, Yosef," Mrs. Diamond said at last. "You know that what they did was wrong. So what can you do? Why can't you tell your principal, Mrs.

Greenberg, about it?"

"Mom, you don't know David and Ari! They'll kill me! They'll know I told. Besides, Mrs. Greenberg never does anything about troublemakers, so why should I go to her now?"

"Why are you so afraid of them? They're the ones who should be afraid, not you!"

Still shaking, Yosef answered, "It's two against one. I could take care of myself and wallop either one of them singly, but together — no siree. You can act brave, but it's me who's gonna get it."

"How can they beat you up during school time?" his father wanted to know.

"How? I'll tell you how," Yosef answered. "In the bathroom, or out during recess when the teachers are busy gabbing, and by the time they notice, it's too late. I know them, Mom. They'll find a way. David's like that. He's mean."

"There must be a way to teach David and Ari that stealing is wrong — and to keep you safe too!" said his mother.

"They know — but they just don't care. We've even been learning about it in class. I don't know why what they learn doesn't mean anything to them."

Holding him close to her, Yosef's mother said, "We love you, Yosef, and we're proud of you. We know you try to be good, and sometimes it's just not easy. But people are like fish in a river. The salmon, and other live fish, fight their way upstream, swimming against the tide. But dead fish don't swim. They just float with the current and are swept away. You want to be a live fish, don't you?"

"Live fish!" exclaimed Yosef, bursting into new sobs. "I just don't know what I'll do!"

"It's late now," Yosef's father said. "Let's go to sleep. Huh? Tomorrow I'm sure you'll have a solution."

Yosef groaned and wrung his hands. His parents hugged him tight and kissed him. "Good night, don't worry," they assured him. "We are sure you'll work it out."

Yosef went back to bed, the words "don't worry," ringing in his ears. "I can't help worrying," he thought. "It's easy to say 'don't worry,' but it's me who's going to get it. But I'm not going to let David and Ari get away with this. If you know about a theft and let it go, it's as bad as being an accomplice! 'Dear G-d,' " he whispered, "please help me find a way to do this. Give me an idea. What should I do?"

After he said his prayer, Yosef felt better. There was nothing he could do about it till morning anyway, and maybe he would be able to think better tomorrow. With these more comforting thoughts, he fell asleep. That night he dreamed that he got all the kids in the class to gang up on David and Ari. They beat them up and got the cards back. He woke up in a sweat and sat up in bed. He thought for a while — then lay back down. "I still don't know what to do."

Eleven

School the next day dragged by. Yosef stayed with his own friends as much as he could, and managed to avoid David and Ari. Recess wasn't a problem, because the boys, as usual, were playing baseball. As Yosef was waiting for his turn at bat, he noticed a boy his own age walking down the street. "Hey, that's Ted," thought Yosef. "I wonder what he's doing out of school. I'll be right back," he told his friends, as he ran to see what Ted was doing at the Talmud Torah.

"I skipped school today," Ted explained. "I wanted to see what your school was like. But I don't see how my Mom's ever going to let me go here. She's going to say, "how can you learn math and science when you're learning Torah half the day?"

"Torah does have math and science," said Yosef, "but a lot more too. But maybe you should just tell her that we have very good math and science classes in the afternoon. Tell her our teachers are good and our classes are small."

"Really?" asked Ted. "She'd like that. And I could tell her I'd be learning Hebrew as a second language. She likes second languages."

"That sounds good," Yosef agreed, patting Ted on the

back. Ted smiled "Thanks, Yos," he said, greatly encouraged. "I'll try talking to her about it again."

"Right," said Yosef. "Keep swimming." At least I don't have the problem of being able to learn Torah, he thought as he ran back to his teammates, I just have the problem of practicing what I learn.

After school, Yosef decided to take a walk. There are four things you can do when you have a problem, he thought. You can think, you can doven, you can ask for advice — and you can go for a walk and try to find an answer. Now, how do you catch a thief? Park Commissioner Elyon was able to find a thief because the thief was sleeping in the morning. Well, what else do thieves do besides sleep in the morning? What sign could David and Ari be wearing that everyone would know that they were the thieves?

Yosef walked a while and thought some more. What experience had he personally ever had with catching thieves? Or that his family had had? No much. Once though, there was a mouse in the house, and Yosef finally caught it. That was a mess. It's probably as hard to catch a mouse as it is to catch a thief, especially if you have a brother like Yoni and like Judah and a sister like Shoni and a mother and father like his mother and father.

"Ehhchchch!" Shoni saw it first, just the tail, actually, as it hurried behind the kitchen counter. "A mouse! The tail of a mouse!"

"How do you know what a mouse looks like?" said

Yoni.

"I know it was a mouse!" cried Shoni. "Ehhchchch! Get rid of it!"

"I know how to catch a mouse," said Yosef. "You set a trap."

"It probably wasn't a real mouse," said Judah. "Maybe it was just a piece of string that looked like the tail of a mouse."

"Pieces of string don't run behind the counter," Shoni insisted. "It *was* the tail of a mouse."

"Maybe it would make a good pet," said Yosef. "White mice cost three dollars at Banderloff's."

"It wasn't white. It was dark grey," said Shoni. "Ehhhchchch!"

Then Yosef's mother came into the kitchen. "Don't make such sounds, Shoni," she said. "What is the matter? Is something rotting under the refrigerator again?"

"A mouse," said Shoni, "I saw its tail!"

"Echchch!" said Mrs. Diamond.

"A mouse?" said Mr. Diamond, coming into the kitchen. "I think we have an old mousetrap in the basement. I'll see if I can find it."

"Do we have cheese to put in the mousetrap?" asked Yosef. "I think I heard they like peanut butter better."

"Cheese is good enough!" said Mr. Diamond, as he went to get the mousetrap.

The trap was a little rusty, so Mr. Diamond put some oil on it.

"Yech," said Shoni. "How can you touch it?"

"How does it work?" asked Yosef.

"Like this," said Mr. Diamond, showing him the spring and the bar and the catch.

"That would *hurt!*" said Yosef.

"Well, mice don't belong in the house," said Mr. Diamond.

"But we aren't allowed to be cruel to animals," said Yosef. "There must be a better kind of trap."

"Well, just now, this is the only one we have," said Mr. Diamond sternly, as he put a small piece of cheese for bait in the trap and gingerly nudged the trap toward the corner. But it went off before it was in place. "These traps are tricky," said Mr. Diamond.

"Let me try," said Judah. "I think it works like — Yiii!"

"You got caught?" asked Yosef.

"You have to be really careful," said Mr. Diamond. "Let me try again."

Finally, the trap was set. The first day nothing happened, except that Shoni wouldn't go into the kitchen because she was afraid she would see a trapped mouse. That night, however, the trap went off. The whole house heard it.

"Euuhh!" exclaimed Shoni.

"Oh," said Judah and Yoni and Yosef. They envisioned a poor little mouse, who was probably hungry, on his way to get a tiny piece of cheese, and now he was caught in the trap with his back broken.

"Oh," said Mrs. Diamond, looking at her husband.

Mr. Diamond looked at the disturbed faces of the rest of his family. "I guess I'll go see," he said at last.

No one said a word. Finally Mr. Diamond's voice broke the silence.

"Look at this," he laughed. "You might as well come see!"

Curious, the family came into the kitchen. The trap had gone off, but it was empty. No cheese, and no mouse.

"I guess these mice are clever," said Mr. Diamond.

"Echch!" said Shoni.

"You need a better kind of trap," said Yosef. "Let me try to find one."

So after school the next day Yosef looked for a mouse trap. He knew that hardware stores sold mouse traps, so he went to examine their merchandise. "Sure," said the man behind the counter. He went and brought out exactly the same kind of trap that the Diamonds had at home, only newer. "We have that kind," said Yosef. "Do you have one that the mice can't take the cheese out of and that won't hurt the mouse?"

The man behind the counter laughed. "Lose your pet, sonny?" he asked. "Well, there is a kind of trap that is a little tray full of resin. The mouse sticks to it. We don't carry it here, though."

So Yosef continued on his way, trying to find another store that might sell resin-type mouse traps. It reminded him of something — then he remembered. Last Purim, when he was looking in the House of Hocus Pocus for a Haman mask with a warty nose, he had passed a counter of gags. And one gag was a box of tissues, and each tissue had some sticky stuff in the middle of it so that it would stick to people's noses. Yosef giggled. Maybe they would have some other gags there that they could use for a mouse trap.

So he went to the House of Hocus Pocus. He was not disappointed. The House of Hocus Pocus featured GETHISOFFAME Glue; the All-Purpose-Trick-Stick, which could be used to make anything stick to any unsuspecting anybody. Yosef bought a bottle of it and spread some on a piece of corrugated cardboard. He then placed his home-made mouse trap near the kitchen counter, where Shoni had seen the mouse. Sure enough, a few hours later little squeaks were heard coming from the kitchen. "All yours, Yosef," said Yoni. So Yosef went into the kitchen and found a frightened little mouse stuck with GETHISOFFAME Glue to the cardboard. "Poor thing," said Yosef to the mouse. "But you don't belong in the house, you know." He took the mouse and trap outside, and shook the mouse out of the trap. The mouse quickly scampered into the grass and was not seen again. "Good work, Yosef," everybody said.

Now Yosef smiled, thinking back on the whole mouse trap incident. It was easier to catch a mouse than a David and Ari, that was for sure. What if he put glue on some baseball cards, and left them on Michael's desk? If David and Ari were going around with baseball cards stuck to their hands, then everyone would know where they got them from. But it wasn't a good idea. First of all, David and Ari were not mice, and they would be able to get the baseball cards off their hands. And anyway, they could always say that they were only picking up the cards to "look" at them.

Yosef walked on and thought some more. He had just learned in class the thirteen rules for learning Torah. One of these rules was that you could take a lesson from something little, a "minor premise" and apply it to something big, or the "major premise." Very good! thought Yosef to himself, as he walked a little bit straighter. Here I am, using Torah to catch a thief — just like Park Commissioner Elyon. Well, the minor premise is that a mouse can be caught in a mouse trap, and such a mouse trap can be bought at the House of Hocus Pocus. Applied to the major premise, that would mean that a David and Ari could be caught in the David and Ari trap, and that that trap could also be found in the House of Hocus Pocus. And that's very good reasoning, because it gives me a chance to go to the House of Hocus Pocus!

Actually, Yosef was already walking in that direction and it only took him a few minutes more to get there.

On this gentle autumn day, the House of Hocus Pocus was really in its glory. An eery whistle blew as you opened the door, and a deep low voice breathed "Wwwelllcommm" Lime green monsters, with bloody daggers piercing through their open wounds, loomed down at you from the higher counters. "Can I help you?" a grizzly bear growled at Yosef(the sales people wore costumes, too). "I want to see the gags," said Yosef.

"Counter four," said the bear.

After first examining some horror faces (it was still a long ways to Purim, but Yosef felt it was always good to know what the selection was), Yosef went over to the gag counter. He remembered some of them from last time. There were the fake glasses that appeared to be filled with juice, but were actually covered with invisible plastic, so that you could never drink anything out of them. There were the little cases that looked like pill boxes, but when you opened them serpents leaped out at you. Then they had some invisible paint that glowed in the dark, that you could paint on the walls to surprise people when they turned off the lights. And here. . .

Yosef looked more closely at a new gag called "Tattle-Fingers." The picture on the label showed an embarrassed looking man trying to hide his fingers, which had turned bright purple. "Know somebody who is too 'touchy' with your things?" inquired the label. "Show him off with Tattle-Fingers print-finger powder. Just lightly sprinkle invisible Tattle-Fingers on your valuable possessions. Invisible on objects, Tattle-Fingers turns bright purple when it contacts fingers. Can not be washed off for many hours."

Of course that was all Yosef needed to know. He

purchased a container of Tattle-Fingers.

"Hey Yosef! What are *you* doing in the House of Hocus Pocus?"

Startled, Yosef turned around. Then he smiled and relaxed. It was Ted. "It's a neat store," he replied to Ted. "Don't you like it too?"

"Sure," Ted responded, "but, what are *you* doing here?"

"Why not?" asked Yosef. "What do you mean?"

"I mean," said Ted, "I didn't think *religious* kids would go here."

Yosef shrugged. "We go here every Purim," he said simply. "You can't get a better Haman mask anywhere. And they have other good supplies here too." Then he told Ted about the mouse, and how he was able to catch the mouse without hurting him with GETHISOFFAME Glue.

"Scary masks and glue," Ted shook his head. "It seems you can get a mitzvah out of anything."

"Yeah," replied Yosef thoughtfully, "maybe you can. Of course, it's fun too." Yosef smiled at Ted, "You know, it's even a mitzvah to have fun doing mitzvahs."

Ted laughed. "Seems like you can't lose," he said.

Twelve

The next morning, Yosef woke up earlier than usual, and dialed Michael's number. "Michael, do you have any more packs of cards?" he asked.

"Yeah," answered Michael sleepily from the other end of the phone. "Why?"

"Just bring them to school with you today. I think I have a way to get back all your cards, *and* find out who the robbers are. I'll explain to you later." Yosef said, and hung up.

When Yosef went to the kitchen for breakfast his mother and father were both there, having breakfast. They were talking before he came in and his father looked very worried about something. As soon as they heard him coming, however, they stopped talking.

"Something wrong?" asked Yosef, reaching for the orange juice.

"It's alright," his father replied. "You look like you're back to your old self this morning. Think of something good?"

Yosef smiled, "Well, let's just say that I'm not floating down with the tide yet," he answered, and his mother smiled, too, as she motioned for him to wash for his grilled

cheese. "You'll do it, Yosef," she said encouragingly. "Keep swimming up that stream!"

Yosef ate quickly and hurried out to the car. Of course, the drive to school seemed longer than usual this morning.

"Can't you speed up a little?" he asked Judah impatiently. "I want to see Michael alone before class."

"Take it easy, I'm going as fast as I can," said Judah. "I really wish I could go faster, Yos, but if we get stopped for speeding, it will take even longer!"

The Taylor chugged on, and finally pulled in to the school drive. "Thanks, Judah," called Yosef as he slammed the car door behind him and raced to catch up to Michael who was just about ready to open the door to the school building. Almost out of breath, Yosef said in a low voice, "Come with me quickly to the bathroom!"

"What's up?" Michael asked, wondering why Yosef was being so secretive.

"I know who took your cards, but you won't believe me. Anyway, I don't want to snitch. So for you to catch them red-handed, I brought this powder. Here, give me the packs of cards, and I'll show you."

Michael handed him the packs of baseball cards. "Like this," said Yosef, as he sprinkled Tattle-Finger powder on the tops of the cards. "Now just be careful not to touch the cards, except on the edge, like this," he showed Michael by holding a pack of cards between his thumb and index finger.

"Leave them on your desk before we go out to recess,

and when we come back you'll know who took them," Yosef assured Michael.

"How will I know? Maybe I'll only be missing more cards," Michael said, biting his lower lip.

"When you notice that your cards are gone, tell Mrs. Snow. Ask her to announce that everyone should raise their hands."

"What good will that do?" Michael asked skeptically.

"The powder turns purple on the skin and can't be washed off for a while," Yosef replied. "It says so on the package. Now come on, let's go to class. Just be careful about touching," he reminded Michael as they headed toward the classroom.

"Thanks, Yos. I just hope you're right."

"Don't worry," Yosef replied confidently, remembering the trapped mouse.

The morning seemed to drag on and on. Every so often Yosef and Michael looked at each other. It was very hard paying attention — it seemed the morning would never end. Finally, the bell rang. Yosef and Michael huddled together during recess. Yosef didn't mention the fact that David and Ari weren't anywhere on the field. Michael didn't notice their absence.

Coming in after recess, sure enough, the cards were not on the desk. Michael glanced at Yosef, and Yosef nodded ever so slightly. Michael looked a little uncertain. He looked again at Yosef, and then turned around and walked to Mrs. Snow's desk. He spoke to her quietly. The class still had not settled down from recess, so nobody noticed. Mrs. Snow listened to Michael. Not understanding why he would want everyone to raise their hands, but wanting to help him in any way that she could, she announced, "Class, would you please sit down, and would all of you please raise your hands?"

Yosef watched David and Ari look at their hands. Purple, bright purple. They looked kind of sick to their stomachs, and were not especially eager to put their hands in the air.

"I said everyone," Mrs. Snow repeated sternly, looking at David and Ari.

The two boys raised their hands, not realizing anyway what it was for.

Michael began shouting excitedly. "They have purple on their hands! See! That's the evidence. They stole my cards. The cards that I brought this morning had powder on them that make your hands turn purple!"

The class was in an uproar. Mrs. Snow went up to David and Ari and motioned to them to follow her. As she was leaving the room, she turned around and said, "Michael, please come with us to Mrs. Greenberg's office."

After school, Yosef and Michael met on the baseball field to pat each other on the back and rejoice over the day's events.

"Did you see the look on their faces when they came back to class?" Michael exclaimed to Yosef.

"Did I ever!" Yosef said. "She really must have given them some talking to!"

"You bet!" said Michael, "They have to replace all the baseball cards, *and* they have to spend an hour after school everyday with Rabbi Golder, learning *laws* which teach about stealing and respecting other people's property."

"Wow!" said Yosef, "just the two of them alone for an hour in a 'class' with Rabbi Golder. They'll have to pay attention."

"Yeah, that was really smart of Mrs. Greenberg," said Michael.

Suddenly they heard someone running behind them. It was Ted. "Guess what!" he panted, as he caught up to them. "I think next week I'm going to start going to your school. Yosef's mom and my mom met at the supermarket the other day, and, Yosef, your mom really told my mom some good things about your school. How good the English program is, and all the special attention that there is, and that each student can go ahead as fast as they want, and that because you get Torah studies too, you don't have to go to any special Hebrew school after school or on Sundays — and she really liked your Mom. So she's ready to let me go now, as soon as I get registered!"

Yosef was really glad, and Michael, who just met Ted, was too. "Great!" said Yosef. "You'll be on our team. And now we can *really* flip cards together, right, Michael!"

The boys spoke happily for quite a while, and when Yosef got home, it was almost dinner time. Mr. Diamond had a worried expression on his face when Yosef walked in, but when he saw the beaming smile on Yosef's face, he put aside his own concerns. "Well, Yosef," he said, "how did it go today?"

"From a minor premise to a major premise!" exclaimed Yosef. "From Gethisoffame to Tattle Fingers!" He tossed the container of powder to his father. "We caught them, Dad. Purple-handed!"

"No fooling!" exclaimed his father, as he examined the Tattle fingers label.

"Yosef? You're home?" called Mrs. Diamond as she came into the room. "What's that?" she asked curiously, but then added, "Come, let's wash for dinner. You can tell us all about it at the table."

So that night at the dinner table, Yosef told them about all the events that happened during the day.

"That was very clever of Mrs. Greenberg to provide an extra study session for the boys," observed Mrs. Diamond. "Now they should really learn their lesson."

"We're really proud of you, Yosef," said his mother.

"Well," said Yosef, "do you remember telling me about how salmon and other fish fight their way upstream, swimming against the tide? And that only dead fish go along with the stream?"

His mother and father nodded.

"Well," Yosef continued, looking down and not at

anyone. "I never forgot that. I always want to be a live fish. That's what I kept thinking about while trying to solve this." Yosef took a deep breath, sat up straight, and raised his eyes. A smile lit up his face as he said, "I'm a live fish!"